# A Time to Reconcile

## A play

## for Children

## 14 Years +

## By George Njimele

"... an exceptional, ingenious work of art whose contribution to contemporary society cannot be overemphasised."

Nganjo Nformi Julius

i

Peacock Writers Series

P.O. Box 3092 Bonaberi, Douala, Cameroon

Tel: (+237) 677 52 72 36

*Email: georgenjimele@gmail.com*

First published 2022

© Peacock Writers Series

ISBN: 978-9956-540-18-1

Book formatting: Nkwain Lawrence B.

Cover design by Theo Mark

# About the author

Njimele was born in Awing, North West Region Cameroon in 1973. He started writing at an early age, and he writes mostly for children and young adults. He took up writing full-time and started the Peacock Writers Series in Cameroon. He won the National Prize for poetry in 1995 organized by the National Book Development Council. Some of his works viz, *Madmen and Traitors* (2015), *The Queen of Power* (1998), *Undeserved Suffering* (2008), *The Slave Boys* (2008) and *Poverty is Crazy* (2012) are prescribed in the Cameroon school curriculum (literature awareness) for beginners in secondary school. His other works include: *King Shaba* (2006), *House of Peace* (2007), *Land of Sweet Meat* (2017), *A Time to Reconcile* (2020), *Reap What You Sow* (2020). His other works, *The Lion and the Tortoise and Other Stories* and *Nyamsi and His Grandson* were selected for the Cameroon/World Bank Read-at-Home Project in 2021. He lives with his family in Douala, Cameroon.

# Table of Contents

# Characters

| | | |
|---|---|---|
| Muluh | – | A coffin maker |
| Malah | – | His wife |
| Beta | – | Their daughter |
| Fineboy | – | Muluh's friend |
| Chato | – | A suitor to Beta |
| Pastor Ako | – | A suitor to Beta |
| Mosi | – | Chato's uncle (a native doctor) |
| Ninta | – | Chato's elder sister |
| Chief Ayago | – | The chief of Elepe |
| A manservant | | |

# ACT ONE

## Scene 1

*In Muluh's house.*

*A frosty morning with noticeable proof of an incoming storm. Malah sits in a sloppy posture in a cane chair. The chair is carefully crafted to lessen her pains when she perches on it. Its arms are lowered and the sitting position widened to make room for more space. Besides concerns of height and space, pieces of woollen fabric in the rear position give the chair a befitting quality of softness. Malah twists her body and her arthritic joints crack audibly.*

Malah:      Ouch! The pains are cropping my flesh…

Muluh:      I see, and you look feeble and depressed. Your health isn't getting any better. What kind of disease is rheumatism?

Malah:      I can't tell. The situation is too gloomy. My legs tingle, twinge and tremble at short intervals. I sense numbness from my waist to my toes. I've become a mobile corpse. In fact, I'm an inch to my grave.

Muluh:      No! Don't invite hell upon your head! I see no danger lurking near or far. By grace or providence, you'll burst out into new health.

Malah:      These are medicines you got for me. *(She shows a polythene bag by her side.)* I respect the dosage, but they barely calm

1

|            | the pains. The twinges keep coming despite my efforts. I abandoned all herbs for these drugs, but nothing better is coming forth. |
|------------|---|
| Muluh:     | Why did you abandon herbal medicine? |
| Malah:     | Ouch! I'm in pains! (*She twists her body.*) They were yielding nothing positive. Some were rather increasing the pains. Ah, what have we not done to dispel this disease? We've sought the help of divine forces. We've made best possible efforts to avoid problems. Despite all, the disease hangs on. It clings on my flesh like black ants. |
| Muluh:     | Go back to the herbs! They will fix the torments of your flesh. The pains won't stay for ever. You haven't committed capital sins anywhere. You don't deserve this kind of suffering. I'm leaving for the market. I have two people in need of coffins. Ah, this situation of yours makes me sick at heart! OK, I'm off! (*He goes in brisk steps. After a while, a deep voice resonates at the door. Pastor Ako approaches glittering with neat and perfectly ironed clothes.*) |
| Malah:     | Welcome, Man of God. (*She grins despite her pains.*) |
| Pastor Ako: | Thank you, Ma'am. May the Lord bless you. |
| Malah:     | Many thanks, Pastor. |
| Pastor Ako: | You still look pale and frail. |

2

| | |
|---|---|
| Malah: | (*She grimaces.*) I'm still in chains, Pastor. I can't describe with mere words what I go through. |
| Pastor Ako: | Mama Malah, the gracious Lord knows everything about your ill health. He won't forsake you. He will not sit and see you perish without being redeemed. |
| Malah: | (*With hands raised in supplication.*) May He hear my prayer! I'm stuck, Pastor. I have tried everything possible. I have nothing to deaden the pains! |
| Pastor Ako: | Do not give up! Only the weak give up in the face of troubles. The devil is putting you to the test. (*He gropes for his wallet, gets a miniature Bible; a sky-blue student version. He flips through the Book and picks a verse of his choice and reads audibly.*) "And it shall come to pass, that whoever shall call on the name of the Lord shall be delivered." |
| Malah: | Amen! (*She bellows.*) |
| Pastor Ako: | Ma'am, don't worry about your flesh. The body is short-lived whereas the spirit is eternal. Your body bears no value; thus don't bother about what to eat or what to wear. Have no fear of sickness. (*He trots up and down, clicking his fingers, smacking his lips.*) |
| Malah: | Thank you, Pastor! I'm very grateful… |
| Pastor Ako: | We thank God, instead! Let's implore the Almighty. (*Malah bows, shuts her eyes and* |

3

*raises her hands piously. It's a long prayer, full of frenetic actions, shouts, a n d emotional outbursts. Malah is used to the rituals. At last, Pastor Ako sways, clasps the Bible in his hands and bounces up and down. Beads of sweat dribble down his cheeks. He paces about, chanting a lyrical hymn.)* How do you feel now?

| | |
|---|---|
| Malah: | Oh, there's much relief than before, Pastor! |
| Pastor Ako: | I'm quite glad to hear that. Where's your husband? |

| | |
|---|---|
| Malah: | He's gone to the market. |
| Pastor Ako: | Ah, I forgot today is the market day. |
| Malah: | It was my place to go there, but illness wouldn't allow me. My husband now keeps house like a devoted wife. And I'm just so glad he does so with a willing heart. |

| | |
|---|---|
| Pastor Ako: | Wow, I'm glad to hear that! He's guided by God to care for your bad health.<br>Ma'am, I have to leave now. I have a prayer session with one of my Christians. Where is Beta? |
| Malah: | She went to have her hair plaited. |
| Pastor Ako: | Say hello to her. |

| | |
|---|---|
| Malah: | All right, Man of God. I'm very grateful. |
| Pastor Ako: | Don't mention it. |

4

# Scene 2

*In Muluh's workshop.*

*Muluh stretches and flexes his arms. He lifts a small-sized coffin and loads up a tricycle. He does same with the second coffin. The latter is a little heavier, crafted with ebony wood. Drops of sweat trickle down his forehead as he struggles with his toilsome task. He relaxes and stands at akimbo, fixes his feet to the ground and sighs. The tricycle rider fastens the ropes that join the coffins to woven steel bars. He steps aboard, ignites the engine. The tyres are heard clunking on both sides as he rides off. Muluh makes for where Beta sits in a carefree mood.*

Muluh:    *(In a solemn tone.)* My dear Beta, lend me your ears. No father will wish his child bad luck. Only a wizard will do so, and most certainly, under a spell.

Pastor Ako has asked for your hand in marriage, and I'm ready to give him the upper hand. I know him full well.

He stands a better chance more than anyone else, because he's filled with the spirit of the Most High.

Beta:    *(Taken aback.)* Ha, he's your choice, not mine! I don't hate him as a person, though. But I can't afford spending a lifetime in the arms of someone I don't love.

He surely has an affection for me; poor him! Advise him to pop the question elsewhere. I won't pity him if he fails in his bidding a thousand times.

5

| | |
|---|---|
| Muluh: | My daughter, be at one with me on this issue. Love does not work the way you think. It grows from the bottom like roots of trees. Then it soars upward in the heart to take a balanced shape. The first priority is to ignite your heart to love someone of the opposite sex. |
| Beta: | (*Resolute.*) I've not ignited my heart to love Pastor Ako. He's a man of God, that's good for him. That's also good for the girl that'll absorb his feelings. |
| Muluh: | You seem not to understand me. As a teen, I know your mind is unripe for the deeper things of love and matrimony. But your mother and I are there to guide you towards a virtuous path. You just have to be obedient and trustful. |
| Beta: | I don't want you to waste valuable time on fruitless efforts. Tell Ako to give up any hope he's nursing. By the way, why can't he come straight and propose to me? Why is he taking shortcuts like a conman? He's timid like a lost pagan. He wishes to marry me, not you. Why then is he wooing you? Are you a girl? |
| Muluh: | (*With a clenched jaw.*) Mind your tongue! I hate unrighteous talks! His approach is OK by me. He isn't out of his mind. He isn't shy either. He wants to seek our approval first. And I consider it the most advisable strategy. Our eyes can see farther than |

|          | yours. When your marriage gets our consent, it stands a good chance of receiving real blessings. |
| Beta: | You mean you won't bless my marriage if it's of my own promptings? |
| Muluh: | (*In a dejected tone.*) I'll bless it with a heavy heart. I'll bless it with half-closed eyes. |
| Beta: | You rather not bless it at all! Why a half blessing? It'll be a faulty blessing, yes! |
| Muluh: | That's my way of denying undeserving love. If you choose to marry a fool, I will not give you my full accord. At the same time, I'll let you know you're swimming in violent waters. To give you real blessings, I must stand by the man that's your heartbeat. Pastor Ako is a humble man with a contrite heart. He has the means to feed you and the children you'll bear. He recently bought a Toyota Camry for private use. His property shall be yours. |
| Beta: | Oh, a car can't move me! Am I marrying him or his car? What if after our wedding, he loses it in a raging fire or in a ravaging accident? The marriage, of course, will be annulled. Yes, indeed, because one of its charms was the car, wasn't it? |

I do not prefer material things to love, Dad.

| Muluh: | Ah, that's good! OK, let us talk more about Pastor Ako. As a child of God, he'll never subject you to violence. With him, you'll not know verbal, mental or physical torture. Some men delight in beating their wives like djembe drums. Will you fancy sharing your roof with such castrated fellows? |
| --- | --- |
| Beta: | Oh, no! I won't dream of it till the end of time. |
| Muluh: | Good! In that respect, Pastor Ako scores a good mark. Witchcraft abounds here, true or false? |
| Beta: | True! |
| Muluh: | Good! Men of God use prayers, fasting, anointing water, sea salt and other things to ward off evil spirits. Under Pastor Ako's roof, you'll know no evil attacks. The owls won't hover and hoot over your housetop. Evil masqueraders, with potent amulets, will not harm you. Totems will bow in your honour. Vampires will take to their heels at your approach. |
| Beta: | Are you exhorting everyone to marry a pastor? How many pastors are there in Elepe? Before the coming of pastors, were your forebears not casting off evil spirits with their own methods? |
| Muluh: | You haven't got my point. I just want you to see the good in marrying Pastor Ako. I'm not a pastor, but I cherish the ways of some pastors. They know how to make and raise |

children. They care for all and sundry. They don't favour the rich, nor do they begrudge the poor. They stand for a just and free society. They bring smiles to the lips of the wretched ones. They are peacemakers and pacesetters. They neither fornicate nor partake in adulterous affairs. They don't frequent motels to trifle with the feelings of underage girls. They don't visit snacks and clubs to indulge in perverse conduct and drunken brawls. They're elegant, smart, and sound in body. They live a life of mutual respect and integrity. From the above aspects, I believe only a Jezebel can resist their proposals.

Beta: Keep me at peace, please! You have a naïve mind! It's embarrassing that at your age you know nothing about your tribesmen.

Muluh: (*Eyebrows raised.*) Oh, you've insulted me!

Beta: I haven't insulted you, Dad!

Muluh: You said my mind is naïve! Withdraw the statement! Withdraw it lest I invoke and deafen you with a peal of thunder!

Beta: I am sorry! I have withdrawn my words.

Muluh: (*With a furrowed brow.*) Ha! In fact, I detest headstrong children. You make me mad as hell! In fact, I prefer breeding dung beetles to breeding children with unbending hearts.

Beta: Heh, I'm not a dung beetle! You, too, have insulted me. But I will not force you to withdraw your words. You are my daddy.

9

|        | That's why you cast dirty words at me as you please. Poor you! Your flaming talks about pastors have fallen on deaf ears. If you wish to marry Ako, feel free! After all, same-sex marriage is on our doorstep. |
| Muluh: | You breathe evil words! You don't screen your words before saying them. So bad for an aspiring wife! A bad-tempered husband will thrash you every day for that. Keep up with the senseless talks! (*He walks away in anger.*) |

# Scene 3

*In Muluh's house.*

Muluh:  It seems the aches have increased again.

Malah:  So badly! This is the most trying day in the history of my bad health.

Muluh:  Hold firm; it'll be over. (*He removes some powdery medicine from his bag, puts it in a cupful of palm oil and stirs with a teaspoon. He rubs her legs with the murky concoction.*)

Malah:  Ouch, it hurts!

Muluh:  That's the healing process.

Malah:  I wish it soothes my pains for good.

Muluh:  It will. Be a little patient and confident.

Malah:  Pastor Ako was here. He prayed with me and asked after you and Beta.

Muluh:  I talked to Beta about him, and she got very angry.

Malah:  (*With lips loose.*) Oh, this little bedbug again!

Muluh:  She expressed disrespect towards Pastor Ako! In fact, we're living real crazy times.

Malah:  Too bad of her! Was your talk about Ako's proposal?

Muluh:  Of course! I opened up to her about it in all sincerity.

Malah:  And what was her say?

11

| | |
|---|---|
| Muluh: | Oh, pride! She burned with wild anger. She intends to go her own way. And at an appointed time, I'll deafen my ears and take it no more. |
| Malah: | I can guess what's happening. For sure, she has taken someone into her heart. |
| Muluh: | And who is that someone, my dear? |
| Malah: | Chato. |
| Muluh: | The naughty boy from Banta, I guess. |
| Malah: | Oh, yeah! |
| Muluh: | My Goodness! Beta has gone out of her mind...! |
| Malah: | I've warned her several times. This fellow keeps prowling like a wild cat, and I've cautioned her against a risky matrimony. When Banta people take to wife an Elepe girl, they treat her like a mean creature. Mindful of this, I asked Beta to avoid this honey-tongued liar. He is a wandering predator. Don't dare marry people who'll trample on your rights without any sense of fear and shame. |
| Muluh: | Banta people hate and prejudice against us. Hate is their greatest legacy. They feel only their own mirrors can give out true reflections. They consider us uncivilised. They demean our cuisine and our outfits. They mock our musical beats and our dance styles. They wed and bang our girls and inflame their eyes. They crunch and |

12

warp their ears and their noses. They say we have thick accent and a small word stock. They despise our birth, marital and funeral rites. They denigrate our craftsmen, our herbalists, our teachers, our musicians, our patrons, and our matrons. They promote and glorify themselves. They lobby and project their own agendas, even when such lack vision and substance. When a Banta man sees an Elepe man, they hunger to disgrace and humiliate him. They derive joy from unholy enterprises . So my dear wife, is that where we want to marry off our daughter?

Malah: A thousand times no! We had better hand her over to a slave than to dare a Banta man. Banta people claim to be superior to us!

Muluh: They aren't! I sold two coffins in the market meant for corpses of Banta people. They die just like us. If they're superior, why don't they defy death?

Malah: They do what we do. Indulging in reckless actions and awkward thinking; chasing women like bees crave nectar; carousing beer like the sharks of the Pacific Ocean; challenging one another to barren fights, et cetera.

Muluh: The Banta people have many lunatics and madmen like us. They have perverted sons and flirty daughters. They have lots of mongols and lepers. Their hospitals are filled with patients struck with incurable

13

ailments. They have deaf, blind, lame, diminutive and obese people. They breathe the very air we breathe. They hock up with women and make children as we do. They hustle daily to earn a living like all of u s Why do they think they're superior then?

Malah: I can't make out anything! They all have black skins like us! In fact, I have cause to oppose this marriage. Period!

Muluh: I stand by your decision. (*The lights dim.*)

# Scene 4

*A dust-laden area in open country. The chirps of birds and howls of beasts are the only signs that life exists here. Two young people stand conversing, now in high spirits, now in low spirits.*

Chato:      Speak your mind, are you for him or not?

Beta:       For whom?

Chato:      For Pastor Ako your good suitor!

Beta:       (*With a neutral look, she laughs derisively.*)
            Who told you he's courting me?

Chato:      Nothing survives in secret for long. I found out myself.

Beta:       If I tell you I intend to marry him, will you believe me?

Chato:      Yes of course! You have the right to make your choice.

Beta:       Oh, God forbid! I can't marry him! He'll force me to join his synagogue. We don't attend the same church, and that's a big issue. He's too old for me. I'm almost half his age. So, he's no match for me! He's loud-mouthed and sharp-tongued. He gives no room for others to talk when he starts talking. He's louder than a tamed parrot. He likes floppy and outdated trousers. He loves sisal-woven hats like cattlemen. He fills his body with bad-smelling perfumes and roll-ons. He loves sleeveless shirts made of bad quality satin fabric. He fancies attires with bright colours; red, yellow, green and

15

orange.

He behaves like countryside fellows. He walks with quick steps like an escapee prisoner. I hate men who bleach; he's one of them! As for his physique, there's nothing desirable about it. He doesn't know how to court and prepare a girl for matrimony. And that's why he uses my parents as a shortcut to get to me. That's ridiculous, isn't it? He's not an apostle of God. He's fake. Anyhow, time will tell!

Chato: (*Very excited.*) OK, do you mean you've tossed out his proposal?

Beta: Yeah! There is no least doubt about that.

Chato: But I learnt he's your parents' choice.

Beta: Heh! They're wasting vital time and energy, washing off the duck's back.

Chato: He has an edge over me because he's an Elepe man. I come from Banta, and your people have an age-old dispute with us.

Beta: He should look for another Elepe girl and marry. I don't love him. I know my parents aren't at one with Banta people. But I truly believe not all Banta people are that bad to merit rejection. And again, I've discovered that many Elepe girls are happily married to Banta people.

Chato: (*With widened eyes.*) These are the sweetest words you've spoken since our love made a

16

|  |  |
|---|---|
| | start. I'm very happy with your reasoning. Another thing he's using to outsmart me is the Toyota car he recently bought, I guess. |
| Beta: | I'm swayed by love, not material things. He'll use his car to influence those who love cars. |
| Chato: | (*Nodding.*) I like your reasoning. I thought you'll debase me because I own a mere bike, and he, a car. |
| Beta: | Ha, not me, please! All said and done, I think your people should be blamed for holding firm to their superior airs. |
| Chato: | I'm one of them, and I won't conceal their lawless tricks and their dubious ways. The truth is sweet when it is said in the nick of time. I don't intend to betray my people to obtain a deed of union with you. My people take pride in the art of enacting joy where there's none. The folly of false pretenses is dangerous; it pushes people to extremes, turns their minds inside out. And that results in chaos and falsehoods. My people excel in various arts amongst which are: backbiting, empty pride, stealing, depraving, coveting, et cetera. The hatred they harbour against others comes from the above sins, which they daily actualise sans mercy. Their fancies are limitless, most often bordering on the things divine powers stand against. They like to demarcate borders where |

17

none exists. Without any aim, they force rivers to flow upstream. They behave like political orators who, after obtaining the mandates, turn against their comrades, plundering their meagre earnings and jailing those opposing bad agendas. I'm one of them, but unique in my own right. I'm not boasting that I carry angelic genes, nor am I claiming to be a prince or a blood relation of any of the major prophets. I believe I'm special in the way I conduct my affairs. One does not need to be a pastor to decode the secret things of God and nature. By careful learning and observation, you'll know how this world works. I like those who speak in tongues, but they mustn't reject me because I don't comply with their routines. They mustn't despise me because I'm not in their assembly. The world is full of countless assemblies that can welcome all flora and fauna.

Beta: That's well said! There's another petty worry I must raise. Your sister may draw the dagger against me in the long run. I met her just once, and our encounter foretold peril. She gave me a long-drawn smile which in my view did not stretch down to her heart. I'm not a mind reader, but facial hypocrisy can't escape my attention.

Chato: Don't mind Ninta. She's not the one marrying you. She's a passive spectator.

18

| | |
|---|---|
| Beta: | As your sister, she has a role to play in your life. The filial link obliges her to oversee and partake in your obligations. |
| Chato: | Oh, no, no! She should entertain her own interests. I don't meddle in her affairs, so she should steer clear of mine. I know her problem. She gullibly engaged in secret love deals with ruthless men. And for the most part, they failed to return her love in equal measure. She got jilted by them till her heart was broken into tiny pieces. She now lives with chagrin and anger. And she's set to avenge herself on any enemy that crosses her bounds. Just any carefree cat, meowing and minding its own business is her victim. She hurls pebbles at it at long range, screaming at its nuisance. Where joy is bubbling, she dashes in uninvited and disrupts it to her delight. She hates merriment, because she has never known any. Her chagrin and cruel actions bear out her long-standing frustration. |
| eta: | Ha, I hope in due course she'll mind her own business. |
| hato: | She has no choice. (*The lights fade* off.) |

# Act Two

## Scene 1

*In a small bar downtown.*

| | |
|---|---|
| Muluh: | My mind is clogged up with fear and doubt. |
| Fineboy: | (*Bewildered.*) Has someone cheated on you? |
| Muluh: | No! |
| Fineboy: | Is someone planning to waylay you? |
| Muluh: | No! |
| Fineboy: | Is someone planning to elope with your daughter? |
| Muluh: | No! But she's the subject of my fear and doubt. She's in a dubious adventure, and all plans may end on a negative note. |
| Fineboy: | Has someone proposed to her? |
| Muluh: | Exactly! Pastor Ako has asked for her hand in marriage, but she judges him an unfit contender. |
| Fineboy: | You have to know these girls are taking far too many liberties. |
| Muluh: | In fact, she wants to drown herself in deep waters. And if it happens, we're all part of a collective suicide. |
| Fineboy: | Has she shown an interest in someone else? |
| Muluh: | Yes; she's offering her heart to a Banta boy! And I'm quite angry at the idea. |
| Fineboy: | Think over it very well! Don't oppose and force her where she'll spend a lifetime as a |

20

|          |                                                                                 |
|----------|---------------------------------------------------------------------------------|
|          | sad and disgruntled wife. Guide her where her heart beats the most. |
|          | But you must give her enough advice. Don't take chances, else she chases the wind in the name of love. Many a girl has plowed destinies into terrible misery because of hasty choices. |
| Muluh:   | My dear friend, don't you think the choice of a Banta boy is ill luck for us? |
| Fineboy: | Banta is not very good, but it isn't very bad either. But you must know marriage is very much like a bazaar game. You have to stake and wait for the result. It's hard to read the conduct of young people today. My lastborn is married in Banta, and she's doing fine. Her elder sister is married to an Elepe man, but her marriage is a strange tale of hell. Whether Elepe or Banta, there are no fixed standards! |
| Muluh:   | Fear is assailing my heart, my dear friend. Banta people aren't in good terms with us. |
| ineboy:  | I had more fear than you when my daughter fell for a Banta boy. I roared like a famished lion, loaded my gun and lay in wait for him. But, at last, their love carried the day, and I joined the dance. I don't regret it, anyhow! I exhort you to give them a try. Banta people won't be our enemies for ever! Many of them have started giving up their claim of superiority. It is a worthless claim, if you ask me. |

21

| | |
|---|---|
| Muluh: | I prefer Pastor Ako to the Banta boy. |
| Fineboy: | You have your reasons which perhaps are faulty in no small way. Do you know much about Pastor Ako? |
| Muluh: | I do. |
| Fineboy: | Perhaps you didn't get me well. Let me repeat my question. Do you know much about Pastor Ako? |
| Muluh: | (*Open-mouthed.*) Your emphasis means things are concealed in the depths of your mind. |
| Fineboy: | I'm no master of slander. I don't want to compromise any betrothal ceremony you intend to organise. If you judge Ako a good suitor for your daughter, bravo! |
| Muluh: | You make me recall something! When I praised Ako, Beta said I have a naïve mind. |
| Fineboy: | Ha-ha! Go ahead, my friend! (*Muluh sits pondering as the lights fade off on them.*) |

# Scene 2

*In Muluh's house*

| | |
|---|---|
| Malah: | (*In low tone.*) Beta, this thing is dragging on for too long. Tell us what lies in the depths of your heart. We need to mend unsettled matters, once and for all.<br>Your love life is chaotic, but a remedy must be found for it. Are you for Pastor Ako or for Chato? |
| Beta: | Mum, I hate boredom. I've spoken my mind before everybody. Why are we harping on this issue? Do we lack work to do? |
| Muluh: | Please, jokes aren't at issue for now! We didn't reach any conclusion yet, did we? |
| Malah: | We didn't, for heaven's sake! Let her tell us why she sees Chato as the treasure of her heart. |
| Beta: | All right! For quite some time now, I have watched him with a keen eyesight.<br>From past to present, there's no scandal on his head. He's not a vain seducer, nor is he an ill-mannered person. He's not reckless in action nor is he lazy in thoughts and feelings. He's sound in mind and body. He doesn't dye his hair with red, green and white colours. He doesn't wear unfastened trousers that hang below the waistline, exposing dirty underwear and a filthy ass. He doesn't smoke addictive tobacco. |

23

|         |                                                                                              |
|---------|----------------------------------------------------------------------------------------------|
|         | He does not take hard or soft drugs like tramadol and cocaine. He avoids swilling alcohol in clubs and bars. He owns five acres of arable land, where he intends cultivating crops and breeding farm animals. |
| Muluh:  | My daughter, when a crook is in desire of something, they cunningly alter their conduct in the short term. Once they get hold of their target, they restore their true nature. Crooks are masters of cajoling tricks. At first glance, they look like old-time angels. They fondly show the best in themselves through fine talks, serene acts and gracious feelings. All of them are the same. Most are pious, and many pious fellows end up as criminal legends. |
| Malah:  | (*Nodding*.) What your father has said does not need any expansion. Your evaluation of Chato may be defective. He may be a crafty chameleon seeking to outsmart and ruin your life. |
| Beta:   | Oh, no! He's the right person for me. He does not raise his voice against elders. When he sees them, he bows and greets them with much adoration. He treats me with tenderness and compassion. In short, he has great respect for women, and on the whole, utmost respect for everyone. |
| Malah:  | You're not immune to games of flattery. A gallant will stop at nothing to snatch the |

|        |                                                      |
|--------|------------------------------------------------------|
|        | girl he fancies most. He might likely use intrigues to his advantage. You know I was married before, don't you? |
| Beta:  | I do! |
| Malah: | My ex-husband was a master of flattery. He was an ill-nurtured, jungle man. He was a snake of vain promises and a mandated liar. I lived with him for eight years without an issue. He blamed it all on me. Meanwhile a physician had earlier diagnosed and duly certified he was sterile. I knew nothing about his medical records. For eight good years, he forced me to drink bitter herbs. I chewed sour and salty leaves. I ate roots of trees, drank parrot blood. I drank donkey urine, ate tortoise excrement, et cetera. He sat gazing at me like a defeated demon. He conspired with his friends and family to blame me at all costs. I later divorced him and met your dad. The second month with your dad I was pregnant! I breathed a sigh of relief! I had been fooled for so long. But there comes a time in life when the truth must come to light. For so long, I was naïve and unripe. Be glad that you have us before you for guidance. Don't fancy and marry a serpent, my daughter. Be wise. The world is full of mischief and betrayal of trust. |
| uluh:  | Do we need to expound what your mother has said? |

| | |
|---|---|
| Beta: | No! |
| Muluh: | And again, marriage here isn't an affair between two persons. You're to marry the entire family, not a single person. Chato may love you like mad; let his success be worth his efforts. He's pursuing a brilliant objective. However, his relatives must give you an equal measure of love, if things have to work in your favour. |
| Malah: | Do you co-operate well with his family? |
| Beta: | Yes, Mum! His uncle and his sister are all for me. |
| Muluh: | Fine, but it doesn't end there! No family is made up of three persons only. You must win over several other members for your side. |
| Beta: | I'm making efforts towards achieving that. |
| Muluh: | Take note; we've not given you the OK yet! |
| Malah: | I'm not sure we'll give her any. She has made a wrong choice. |
| Beta: | (She *grimaces and rolls her eyes.*) I've met no wrong choice! (*She goes off half angry.*) |

# Scene 3

*In the palace of Chief Ayago. A gleam of light reveals a royal chamber, adorned with antiquities and awe-inspiring skins of beasts. Pastor Ako is ushered into the chamber by a manservant. He settles and greets the chief with courtesy.*

Pastor Ako:   Greetings, Your Highness.

Chief Ayago:   Welcome.

Pastor Ako:   Your Highness, I'll start by praising your vow to uphold peace and order in a place teeming with big problems. Our land boils with danger created by lawbreakers. I mean individuals badly brought up by sick minds. This is an uncertain society with twisted laws and invented happiness. I'm not by this criticising your leadership skills.

Chief Ayago:   Welcome, my friend. Even if you criticise me to my face, that won't split up my heart. A good ruler leads with the wisdom of unbiased critics. I only act in conformity with powers bestowed upon me by my ancestors. I'm loyal to those who mandated me to rule. It's no easy duty, but I do my best to serve every interest, high or low. My duty is by far too complex than you can figure out.

Pastor Ako:   Your Highness, such exacting duties need the support of a divine hand. And as I have always said, you can't succeed without engaging God in your daily tasks.

27

| | |
|---|---|
| Chief Ayago: | You're very right! Whenever I invoke my ancestors, I always end by linking them up with the Almighty. He's the ultimate shield above anything. I don't ignore His role, so to say. |
| Pastor Ako: | Your Highness, I feel offended when you keep giving the pride of place to departed souls. In my opinion, these ancestors ought to play second fiddle in your life.<br><br>I honestly think they're dead and gone afar. They lie in skeletal shapes in their burial places… without mind, without soul, with no body. Let's ignore them and push ahead the mission of the living God. |
| Chief Ayago: | As a pastor, I know your worries. But, we won't belabour any point now! You're a peace crusader. Bravo! However, certain facts about the inner truths are bound to escape your mind. Your belief is imported. And, all imported ideas are altered along the way to suit certain whims. Anyhow, that kind of debate is not for now. Let's put it off for another time. I like the role you are playing. Without any pretence, I commend your job. If I were against you, I would've long proscribed your activities. I have the necessary powers to act where the interest of this land is at stake. You're doing your job, and I'm doing mine. You miss the point by trying to grasp the details of my real |

28

nature. You are not initiated to observe and understand the sacred truths of this place. This is a chiefdom with core agendas. In brief, the common purpose is upholding the truth, protecting rights, lives and property. We tune to various melodies, but dance in the same direction. That said, let's explore the subject of your visit.

Pastor Ako: Your Highness, a vexed mind is much like a kingdom of tears. My heart bleeds. Not that I lack the faith to endure my troubles! It's due to the fact that my troubles haven't got enough attention in high places.

Chief Ayago: You've not brought them to my notice. How do I resolve issues you've not tabled before me? A cock offers its prey to the hen to reveal its intentions.

Pastor Ako: Your Highness, I thought as the overseer of the land, you're conscious of the petty troubles aching our hearts.

Chief Ayago: I know about certain problems. But I can't know everything! It's not possible for one to know everything. No one is obliged to be all-knowing. Even the most efficient diviner can't foretell future events with watertight accuracy. Only the Almighty God has such powers!

Pastor Ako: Your Highness, there's an alien boy with raving manners in our land. He has come here with nothing but evil intentions. He is a stray he-goat.

Chief Ayago: Who's he?

29

| | |
|---|---|
| Pastor Ako: | Chato is his name! An owl flying about in daylight. He has no property to his name. |
| Chief Ayago: | I know him. He's from Banta, isn't he? |
| Pastor Ako: | He is, Your Highness. For heaven's sake, blacklist and banish this fellow from here now! |
| Chief Ayago: | What charges do you hold against him? |
| Pastor Ako: | Your Highness, Elepe is not his birthright. To be precise, he comes from Banta. Instead of being humble as a foreign boy, he sets about using queer ways to obtain favours and benefits here. Let him return to his fatherland where sin is highly valued. |
| Chief Ayago: | Now, now, I don't buy your idea! As a chief, I don't promote tribal hatred. I'm the leader of the Elepe people, and also the leader of strangers willing to settle and live here. Strike that point off and bring forth another which is worthy of sanction. |
| Pastor Ako: | Your Highness, this notorious ex-convict stands in the way of all my efforts. I have pledged to marry Muluh's daughter with good intention. Ha! At the speed of light, he proposed to the very lady to frustrate my ambition. |
| Chief Ayago: | The fact that you were first to propose to her didn't give you any priority over other suitors. Marital engagement isn't a matter of first come, first served. It's a love game. If the lady does not love you, it's her right to select a different contender in the race for |

30

|  | her heart. If I may ask, was she in your favour? Did your words put smiles on her face? |
|---|---|
| Pastor Ako: | Yes, Your Highness! And her parents judge me as a precious stone, the saviour of the family.<br><br>They foresee me as an in-law that'll make them suck nectar, drink unadulterated palm wine, lick butter and eat sweet meat. |
| Chief Ayago: | Now, how's Chato blocking your goal? |
| Pastor Ako: | As he saw me on the verge of success, he jumped in with all kinds of roguery frauds. He's bent on spilling venom on all my plans. Sensing defeat at the initial stages, he began staging danger against me. Twice, he attempted to set our synagogue ablaze. He sent his ex-convict friend to poison me, but the Lord shamed their action. He asked my followers to boycott our worship days, calling me a fake choirmaster. Yet, none of my converts heeded his satanic call. After many countless failures, his latest plan is to waylay and assassinate me. That's his most cruel move to stop me from breathing…to render me a martyr or a saint, as the case may be. Your Highness, that's why I think this roving cockerel has no place amongst civilised people. He'll invite Lucifer here! |
| Chief Ayago: | Ha! This matter spells grave danger indeed! I didn't imagine it to have gone this far. OK, I've heard your own say. I'll investigate him. As a matter of urgency, I'll summon him here to give his own side of the story. |

| | |
|---|---|
| Pastor Ako: | Your Highness, I fear for my life. If that daring bandit takes my life, there'll be a huge vacuum in the church community here. The peace and love I've tactfully restored with the Gospel will vanish. Your Highness, you can't overlook my worth here. I'm too worthy to be slain because of a woman. I refuse to trip and fall like Adam! |
| Chief Ayago: | Your case is on the front burner of charges to be considered soon. |
| Pastor Ako: | Your Highness, I count on your sense of justice. Save the life of God's faithful and tireless apostle. |
| Chief Ayago: | My duty obliges me to act in accordance with the law where need arises. You'll lose no drop of your blood to any pitiless slayer. *(Pastor Ako exits and goes off.)* |

# Scene 4

*In Chief Ayago's palace.*

*A faint voice echoes offstage, announcing the appearance of Chato in Chief Ayago's palace. The palace has an improvised courthouse in its rear (built in a calm and noiseless area.) There are two docks with short-length tables, no seats for the audience. The hall gives out dim, pub-like lights from halogen bulbs. Chato is ushered into the courthouse by a manservant. After a couple of minutes, Chief Ayago walks in and seats himself in a wicker chair fronting the dock. He's the sole chief judge for the day's hearing. Without any fuss, he begins the court session.*

| | |
|---|---|
| Chief Ayago: | *(In an uplifted voice.)* What's your name? |
| Chato: | Chato Chindo, Your Highness. |
| | |
| Chief Ayago: | What's the name of your tribe? |
| Chato: | Banta, Your Highness. |
| Chief Ayago: | What brought you to Elepe? |
| Chato: | I came here for work, Your Highness. |
| Chief Ayago: | What kind of work do you do? |
| | |
| Chato: | Farming, Your Highness. I'm a crop cultivator. |
| Chief Ayago: | Have you been to prison before? |
| Chato; | No, Your Highness. |
| Chief Ayago: | *(Downcast; eyes wide open.)* Let me ask you the question again! Have you ever been imprisoned anywhere? |

| | |
|---|---|
| Chato: | No, Your Highness! I've never been charged with crime anywhere. |
| Chief Ayago: | (*He casts stern looks at Chato.*) Do you know Pastor Ako? |
| Chato: | Yes, I do, Your Highness. |
| Chief Ayago: | What do you think about him? Is he cruel, dubious or fake? |
| Chato: | Your Highness, I know very little about him. |
| Chief Ayago: | Come on! Tell me the little you know about him. Is he any good? |
| Chato: | First, I know he's a pastor. Second, we both have proposed to the same girl. |
| Chief Ayago: | What's the name of the girl? |
| Chato: | Beta, Your Highness. |
| Chief Ayago: | Whose daughter is she? |
| Chato: | She's the daughter of Muluh Kwato. |
| Chief Ayago: | From the look of things, can you bet you'll win Beta's love? |
| Chato: | It's a difficult question, Your Highness. I'm not in her mind. She'll make her choice in due course. |
| Chief Ayago: | Is there anyone else proposing to her apart from the two of you? |
| Chato: | There's none as far as I know. But I'm not one hundred percent sure. |

| | |
|---|---|
| Chief Ayago: | Tell me. Do you hate the Pastor because he intends to marry Beta? |
| Chato: | No, Your Highness! |
| Chief Ayago: | Be frank with yourself. Even if you don't hate him, you should be angry with him for wanting what you desire. Tell me the truth. Don't hide your feelings from me... |
| Chato: | Your Highness, I must confess; sometimes I fear I may be the loser. All the same, I consider this a game of chance. Anyone can win when the time for winning is due. I've kept a level head all along. |
| Chief Ayago: | Has it occurred to you that doing away with Pastor Ako will multiply your chances of taking Beta to wife? |
| Chato: | (*a little in shock.*) No, Your Highness! That'll be the worst crime to commit. I don't want to spend a lifetime |
| reading | prison corridors. |
| Chief Ayago; | What if you commit the crime and you aren't found out? |
| Chato: | Your Highness, if anything happens to Pastor Ako now, I'll be the main suspect. And I can't go free. I'm on the battlefront with him over love! |
| Chief Ayago: | Do you know where his church is found? |

35

| | |
|---|---|
| Chato: | No, Your Highness. |
| Chief Ayago: | Have you had the chance to talk to some of his followers? |
| Chato: | No, Your Highness. I'm busy with my farm work. I know very few people here. |
| Chief Ayago: | Do you have any friend who has served a prison term? |
| Chato: | No, Your Highness. |
| Chief Ayago: | What do you know about poison? In a word, do you know any medicine that can be used to poison someone? |
| Chato: | No idea, Your Highness. |
| Chief Ayago: | Oh, let's be frank here! Do you want me to believe you know nothing about poison? |
| Chato: | I know a bit about poison, but I don't like discussing about it. |
| Chief Ayago: | Why? |
| Chato: | Poisoning someone to me is the cruelest thing imaginable! |
| Chief Ayago: | How do you feel when you learn someone has died through poisoning? |
| Chato: | (*In a grimace.*) I feel devastated! |
| Chief Ayago: | How do you feel when you learn someone is ambushed and assassinated? |
| Chato: | Oh, my mind is broken! The horror of death blasts my heart! |
| Chief Ayago: | Come and write down the names of your most intimate friends. Just two names. |

|              |                                                                                                  |
| ------------ | ------------------------------------------------------------------------------------------------ |
|              | State where they live and the names of their parents. (*Chato gets a pen and writes in neat handwriting.*) |
| Chato:       | Is it OK?                                                                                         |
| Chief Ayago: | It's OK! You can go now! Somehow, I'll still investigate you in the days ahead.                   |
| Chato:       | Thank you, Your Highness! (*Happy, he goes off.*)                                                 |

# Act Three
## Scene 1

*In Muluh's house.*

*A human shadow emerges from one end of the stage. As it advances, it starts revealing recognizable features. Malah observes it, turns and strikes a nuisance fly on her kneecap. She remains in her posture. The man in the shadow is none other than Pastor Ako. He walks past the doorpost and sits on the chair astride. He's slightly confident in himself. He wears a gorgeous green suit, which is neatly ironed and is stiff with more than enough starch.*


| Pastor Ako: | Madam, you look unwell and unbalanced. |
| Malah: | Yes, Pastor! |
| Pastor Ako: | Ma Malah, you lack faith! You make light of your condition as if you invited it by yourself. You're accepting undue defeat. May God pardon you for that. |
| Malah: | No, Pastor! I'm for the Lord and the Lord is for me. |
| Pastor Ako: | Then you shouldn't be in pains. When the Lord takes your life under His control, your prayers are listened to. With a simple fast, that nagging disease will disappear. (*Muluh enters.*) |
| Muluh: | Ha, the chosen one! Welcome, my Lord! |
| Pastor Ako: | (*Grinning.*) Ha! The sole in-law I know. |

|  |  |
|---|---|
|  | The number one granddad of my future kids. |
| Beta: | (*Aside. Mimicking offstage.*) Ugh! In-law my foot! I hate you with every fibre of my being! Marry them, idiot! |
| Pastor Ako: | I'm telling Ma Malah to stop taking drugs. She should pray to get healed. |
| Muluh: | Man of God, we pray day and night… |
| Pastor Ako: | You don't pray with conviction. You pray like a toddler making fun with a doll. What results do you expect with that? |
| Malah: | I solemnly promise to engage more in prayers, Man of God. |
| Pastor Ako: | Do so without looking backward. You'll bustle about like excited teenagers. Heaven will heal you. |
| Muluh: | I'll personally supervise her prayers. |
| Pastor Ako: | Very good! Where's Beta my love? |
| Malah: | She's not far away. She was here not long ago. |
| Muluh: | Beta! (*He shouts. In an aside, Beta starts singing offstage. She intones a love song and sings. Her soft voice reverberates on nearby surfaces. Afterwards, she continues to eavesdrop on her parents.*) |
| Malah: | She isn't far away… |
| Muluh: | Perhaps she saw Pastor and hid herself somewhere. |
| Pastor Ako: | That brings us to real issues now. My dear |

39

|            |                                                                                 |
|------------|---------------------------------------------------------------------------------|
|            | in-laws, If I take an interest in your child, it's because I hold you in esteem. And I think none of you bears a grudge against me. |
| Malah:     | Heh! A grudge, for what reason, Pastor?                                          |
| Muluh:     | (*With emphasis.*) You're the true son of the soil! That alone avails all your projects here. You'll make a righteous son-in-law. |
| Pastor Ako: | My dear in-laws, let's present facts as they are. You're lenient and lacking in focus. Beta is the only child you have, are you with me? |
| Malah:     | (*Listening seriously.*) That's very true.                                       |
| Pastor Ako: | If I'm not overstating my point, I think Beta should be the pillar of your hopes. |
| Muluh:     | She is, Man of God.                                                              |
| Pastor Ako: | She is the only child, and the only thing you can't stake. You can't auction her to a slave boy, can you? |
| Malah:     | Not in the least! You speak logical words, Man of God!                           |
| Pastor Ako: | How can you bait, catch a fish, then you rinse it in water?                      |
| Muluh:     | Man of God, I get you well. We must figure out this issue. You've been our very first choice, and as it stands, we still uphold you. |
| Malah:     | We reserve for you the place of honour, Man of God.                              |
| Pastor Ako: | A lazy dog does not deserve a juicy piece of meat!                               |

40

| | |
|---|---|
| Muluh: | You're right! It deserves the hardest bones. |
| Pastor Ako: | That young man is from Banta. That alone devalues him in any contest with me. I'm a son of the soil. I'm an anointed apostle. I'm an enlightened servant of God. I own a synagogue, I own a beautiful car and a splendid villa. I have invested in real estate. And I intend to invest in fishery and cattle. I'm of noble birth. I'm ripe, bright, wise and rational. I have the means to take care of my needs. Who knows him? Whose son is he? Let him recount his own credits. I don't compete with hungry vagabonds! |
| Beta: | (*Aside*.) Oh, what a braggart! Look at him! Ha! And he calls himself a Man of God! |
| Malah: | He is no match for you, Man of God! |
| Muluh: | Pastor, you wield real power and honour... |
| Malah: | To God be the glory...Halleluiah...oooh! |
| Pastor Ako: | At times, when a child is sinking in a messy hole, we must use a big whip to set her conduct straight. To correct a child, you have to overlook certain rules of justice, and the media babbles about children's rights. Beta is making a wrong choice. She's forcing herself into the arms of a vagabond. That boy will sooner or later turn into a hardened robber! I've briefed the chief on this wrong presage. My in-laws, let's reason well. At any moment, that roving cockerel will be exiled from this land. I have already worked out the plan with Chief Ayago. |

41

| | |
|---|---|
| | (*Beta dashes in with a pestle in hand and makes to strike Pastor Ako.*) |
| Muluh: | (*His mouth stretched, he springs to his feet and shouts at the top of his voice.*) Stop it! (*Pastor Ako rises on time and flees towards a safe exit. Beta pursues him, her pestle at the ready. She continues her chase and the Man of God bursts out panting, scuttling and letting out a loud wail. His s h a d o w fades off in the distance. His hat, muffler and brochure are scattered on bare ground.*) |
| Malah: | (*Scandalised, mouth hanging open.*) What's this? Have you gone insane? |
| Muluh: | (*Breathing uneasily, his lips tightened, his eyebrows pulled down.*) I didn't know you could be that ferocious! Strike me with the pestle! Strike me! (*He rushes forth and crashes into her, grips her firmly. Beta struggles and breaks away, recoils and goes off. The lights fade off on the scene.*) |

# Scene 2

*In Muluh's house.*

*Enter Chato and his uncle Mosi. Chato is carrying a ten-kilo antelope in a cane basket. He jerks an arm, descends the basket onto his shoulders. Then he hunches his shoulders, lowers the basket and lays it on a flat wood. Malah sits tilted, eyeing her visitors warily. The antelope has just been freshly killed. Weird blood is dribbling from its nostrils. Chato and Mosi settle. Mosi looks elderly, scaly in the face, slightly stooped. He has grey moustache, walks with the help of a staff. He carries a fibre bag with a strap over his shoulder, his arm looped through the strap. The bag is brown with age.*

| | |
|---|---|
| Malah: | (*With a neutral face.*) I am glad to see you. |
| Mosi: | Thank you, Ma'am. |
| Chato: | This is my uncle. He came all the way from Banta. |
| Malah: | (*Gazing at Mosi.*) OK. I can see how you resemble him. How is Banta? |
| Mosi: | Very fine, Ma'am. Everybody is in sound health. |
| Malah: | (*She twists her body.*) It's been long I've not set foot in your tribe. With this illness I hardly move. I've become a cocooned insect; a young bird confined in its coop. |
| Mosi: | My son told me about your ill health. And |

43

|          | that's one of the reasons I have come here. |
|----------|---------------------------------------------|
| Malah:   | Ah, are you a native doctor? |
| Mosi:    | Yes, Ma'am. And I'm adept at treating rheumatism. |
| Malah:   | That's what dozens of native doctors have been telling me. They all come claiming to be specialists. They make efforts, but I cannot see any results. Pitiful, indeed! |
| Mosi:    | No two specialists are the same. I'm not boasting about my abilities. But just give me a little bit of trust. Ma'am, you'll be fine in a couple of days. |
| Malah:   | *(Glares at him with disbelief.)* I'll only trust you if I'm healed. |
| Mosi:    | *(Reaches for his bag and pulls out some liquid medicines in a bottle. He gets powdery medicines and ointments too and lays them on the floor.)* |
| Muluh:   | Hmmm! You emptied your temple! |
| Mosi:    | *(His face shines with a divine smile.)* You'll get healed sooner than expected! |
|          | *(He instructs her on dosage and length of treatment.)* |
| Malah:   | Thank you very much. I will follow the dosage accordingly. |
| Mosi:    | When my son told me you suffer from rheumatism, I felt so sad. I said to myself, that's a small matter. That's a disease I'll kick out with my left foot. |
| Malah:   | Really? |

44

| | |
|---|---|
| Mosi: | Yeah! You'll get well in no time. He also told me something very special. He said he has come across a ripe banana in your backyard, and has taken an interest in it. |
| Malah: | Ah, that's amusing! Why does he take an interest in something that's not his? |
| Mosi: | He knows it's for someone else. But out of goodwill or generosity, the owner may decide to spare it. |
| Malah: | Ha! In any case, my husband isn't at home. I can't by myself handle such talks in his absence. You have to come back some other time for proper talks. |
| Mosi: | There's no problem, Ma'am. We'll fix a rendezvous for that. |
| Malah: | That's it! (*Looking at the cane basket.*) I can see a large animal in the basket. What's it? |
| hato: | It's an antelope, Ma'am. |
| Malah: | Ah! What's it for, my son? |
| Mosi: | (*In a soft voice, smiling.*) It's an ordinary gift, Ma'am. You'll roast it for your meal. |
| Malah: | Well, I won't ask you to go back with it. I'll keep it. When my husband returns, I'll show him and tell him what you've said. If we deny you the ripe banana in our backyard, we'll return your meat. If we've eaten the meat before then, we'll offer you |

something else in replacement of it. I'm simply trying to make myself understood, are we OK?

Mosi: I get you quite well. As you've said, we'll keep our fingers crossed. I'm very certain we'll have the banana for ourselves.

Malah: I wish you good luck!

Mosi: No worries, Ma'am. I wish you a speedy recovery. (*They exit. Beta enters.*)

Malah: Hmmm, have a look at my medicines. The battle for your heart is fierce and exciting.

Beta: (*Ignores what her mum has just said. Looking at the basket with curious eyes.*) What's this?

Malah: Ha, an antelope, my daughter! Antelope...!

Beta: Oh, this is quite cool! Your big-time pastor couldn't offer you a bush rat! He spent all his sober moments talking, with nothing good coming out of his talks. Look at the gains of a first visit! It's simply amazing! I told you these people are worth dealing with. A fleshy bush animal to relish an evening meal! Then medicines for your disease! What else could be more delightful than this?

Malah: You have a point. I now see the logic in your appeals to us. I'll think better of this encounter. Actions speak louder than words. When your father comes back, we'll study this matter in minute detail.

| | |
|---|---|
| | But I'm against your actions of the other day. I told you that before. You acted like a murderer in the pay of an enemy. |
| Beta: | Put yourself in my shoes. You're alive and strong in mind and spirit. Then someone closes in on you to ruin your love life. Would you fold arms, sit by him and drink a toast to his merrymaking? |
| Malah: | Good question! What do I do in a similar case? I shout out at my enemy and maintain my calm. That's not what you did. You chased him with a pestle. |
| Beta: | I wanted to put him in fright, and I think my entire mission was achieved. I know he left in anger and regret; he had the right to that. And I bet you, he will never dare my temper again. |
| Malah: | Never repeat that kind of display in your life. I took you for a killer. I could hardly admit you came from my womb. |
| Beta: | Badly managed anger leads to bad actions. A few moments after the action, I sensed guilt flowing in my blood. That meant my intention was of half measure. All the same, he sprang to his feet like a runaway clown. |
| Malah: | You had your heart sweetened with his disgrace, I guess. |
| Beta: | For sure! |
| Malah: | Are you convinced you paid him in his own |

|  |  |
|---|---|
|  | coins? |
| Beta: | I am, obviously! He won't dare me anymore. |
| Malah: | My daughter, subdue your heart and avoid bad actions! That man is an apostle of God! |
| Beta: | Have your medicines, Mum. We're walking on good footpaths. |
| Malah: | (*She gets her medicines and starts drinking some, rubbing some, and chewing others according to dosage instructions. Beta removes the dead animal from the basket and lays it on a mat. She steps back and eyes at it. The scene blacks out slowly.*) |

# Scene 3

*At a crowded checkpoint.*

*A beautiful girl in her late twenties walks onstage. She's slim, has narrow eyebrows, dark lashes, a narrow face, a narrow nose, high cheekbones, and puffy lips. She is well clad in a well -fitted blue jeans and a white tricot. She wears a pair of tennis shoes and a flat cap. She's soft-spoken, romantic and sturdy. She has plump legs and a rounded bottom. She meets Beta at the checkpoint and swoops onto her in frenzy.*

Ninta:      (*Embracing Beta in a tight grip.*) Oh, you look beautiful! What a wonderful creature for my brother!

Beta:       (*In a shy mood.*) Thank you, I'm pleased to see you.

Ninta:      I came to greet and have a chat with you. Is your mum getting better?

Beta:       Yeah! Your uncle gave her medicines, nice medicines. Yesterday, I saw her walking unaided for the first time since she took ill.

Ninta:      Wow, I'm so glad to hear that! How's your dad?

Beta:       He's fine.

Ninta:      Our meeting will be very brief. This is just a casual visit. I'll see your parents some other time, most probably, during an official meeting.

Beta:       There's no problem.

49

| | |
|---|---|
| Ninta: | I'm glad to see you. My brother has talked to me about you. He informed me he has proposed to you. I like the idea. You'll be part of us. And I, too, will soon be part of you. (*She smiles at Beta.*) |
| Beta: | He, too, talked to me about you, but not in detail. |
| Ninta: | I'm kin to him, his elder sister, to be very brief... I breastfed before him, and he respects me for that. (*Chuckling.*) |
| Beta: | Ha-ha, I like that! |
| Ninta: | I mentioned a while ago that I'll be part of you. This means two things… and I guess you didn't quite understand me. Obviously, with this marriage, we're one. That's the first fact. But there's another fact; good news, of course!<br>(*She widens her eyes and winds her waist in excitement.*) |
| Beta: | I will be pleased to hear the good news. |
| Ninta: | I'm engaged to an Elepe man! A handsome, kindly man. Therefore, as you're moving to Banta, I'm moving to Elepe. |
| Beta: | Wow! What a coincidence! |
| Ninta: | So, have no fear! I forgive the cynical boys who frustrated my life without pity. I'm a happy girl now! Sadness is for the past. No more sorrow and grief! At last, someone has got hold of my heart. Someone saw the good in me and heaped his trust in me. |

|        |                                                                 |
|--------|-----------------------------------------------------------------|
|        | I'm more than happy!                                            |
| Beta:  | So am I!                                                         |
| Ninta: | I'll miss you for a while. Anyhow, you'll see me here very often. Please, my dear wife, I'll leave you now. But not without a small token... It's a little sign of bigger things on the way. There are best moments ahead... Take care! (*She puts her smooth arms round Beta's neck and hugs her. She offers Beta a skirt, a party gown and a pair of low-heeled shoes.*) |
| Beta:  | (*Cheeks raised.*) I'm very grateful. (*She stands transfixed, admiring her gifts. They part ways, and the lights dim gradually.*) |

## Scene 4

*In Chief Ayago's palace, at the approach of sunset.*

| | |
|---|---|
| Chief Ayago: | (*With a stern face.*) Pastor Ako, I hate one who tells lies! You are mature enough to set up an innocent young man for selfish gains. |
| Pastor Ako: | What's the matter, Your Highness? |
| Chief Ayago: | You levelled false accusations against Chato. He has never been to prison as you declared. He's not an ex-convict. You told a falsehood against him. You defamed him. If charged, you you'll be found guilty of defamation and that's punishable by law. You will be liable to a jail term for telling improbable lies. |
| Pastor Ako: | Your Highness, the information was relayed to me by a third party. |
| Chief Ayago: | And did you verify its validity? Did you, Pastor? |
| Pastor Ako: | Your Highness, I admit my mistake. To err is human, to forgive is divine. In fact, I regret this. I didn't mean to destroy his image because of self-interest. |
| Chief Ayago: | It's surprising but true. You wanted to crush Chato with clever tactics. I'm |

the chief of this place. I'm used to such manoeuvres. It's shameful, I must admit! You framed up stories to weaken your rival. Your tales about poisoning and murder were invented. I see a lot of bad faith in your accusations against him. I went down to Banta and investigated Chato. I inquired about him from several people. He's not a criminal. There's no criminal record against his name. Your stories were fabricated, Pastor Ako. And I'm not happy with you at all! Anyway, as custom demands, you'll be fined for propagating slander and false testimonies. In that respect, I expect you here tomorrow with three he-goats and four cocks. I'm less strict on you, somehow. Next time, you won't believe my action! This fine will wash away the falsehood you told against this innocent young man.

Pastor Ako: Your Highness, I'll do as you command… (*He exits, striking his neck with guilt. About six hours later, he reappears.*)

Chief Ayago: I asked you to pay the fine tomorrow and not today!

Pastor Ako: Your Highness, this is a burning issue! It demands a prompt reaction!

Chief Ayago: (*He makes forward and inspects the goats*

*and the cocks.)* This goat is undersized. Anyhow, I won't oblige you to replace it. The cocks are sizeable; that's good! Now, tell me, are you sure of winning the Banta boy in this love battle?

Pastor Ako: Your Highness, I've given up already. Beta is a beast! She almost took away my life last week. She'll end up in hell, I bet you!

Chief Ayago: Heh, don't tell me Beta can slay someone!

Pastor Ako: I visited them and sat conversing with her parents. Suddenly, she leapt onto us from nowhere, carrying a pestle, big enough to weigh two tons. She lifted it up and set pursuing me, ready to strike me with it. I survived her attempt on my life by a stroke of luck. From that day, I terminated all contacts with her. To say the least, she's evil incarnate!

Chief Ayago: That's very bad news! It shows she does not love you at all.

Pastor Ako: Even if she loves me now, I will never reciprocate her love. The love I had for her has evaporated!

Chief Ayago: Her show of violence was a bad sign. It means while in your home, she'll use the pestle on you anytime.

Pastor Ako: Your Highness, that's true. And that's why I've terminated all contacts with her. I don't

|  |  |
|---|---|
|  | want to house a serpent in the name of a wife. I can't bear her soldierly attitude... |
| Chief Ayago: | I suppose they'll refund all the gifts you offered them during courtship. |
| Pastor Ako: | Your Highness, I've not lost one dime in this affair. She has not taken one franc of my money. I doubted everything right at the beginning. |
| Chief Ayago: | Hmmm, sometimes you need to lose in order to gain. Offering her gifts could have sweetened her heart and increased her interest in you. Maybe you failed because your strategy was not good enough. You can't catch fish without using a tackle. |
| Pastor Ako: | Ah, let it be so! I've lost nothing, and I'm OK with that. She's not even a born again Christian. Perhaps that's why she acts like a devil. Truly, God has kept me out of danger. I'm in search of a God-fearing wife, not a reckless butcher! |
| Chief Ayago: | I wish you good luck! |
| Pastor Ako: | Many thanks, Your Highness. (*Lights fade.*) |

# Scene 5

*In Muluh's house.*

| | |
|---|---|
| Muluh: | My dear, you look very cheerful and robust. |
| Malah: | (*Her face beams with joy aplenty.*) I've fully regained my health. With this healing, I can only wonder what will come next. A good chance has come to me, but I'll stay true to myself as always. Ah, my husband, smiles have visited me at the right time. Have a taste of what I can do now. (*She springs out of her seat and walks across the sitting room with ease.*) |
| Muluh: | (*Amazed.*) Wow, this is marvellous! It's unthinkable! Mosi deserves a kola from us. |
| Malah: | Kola plus other benefits, of course! Ha, gnawing pains for four years running...! |
| Muluh: | It has been a bitter pill to swallow! Mosi is a worthy native doctor. |
| Malah: | There's still a fair share of the antelope meat left. |
| Muluh: | I'll like to eat supper with it. It's sweet venison, indeed. |
| Malah: | Beta will roast, salt and pepper it for you. |
| Muluh: | Now, let's close the issue between her and Chato. What's your take on it for now? Please, we must avoid divided opinions. |
| Malah: | We owe a debt of thanks to Mosi for curing me of my disease. We're grateful to Chato for his undivided love towards our daughter. We also thank Mosi for the gift of doing the |

|         |                                                              |
|---------|--------------------------------------------------------------|
|         | right thing at the right time. He has done a great job by restoring my health. We thank him, too, for the antelope; its juicy meat in particular. |
| Muluh:  | You forgot Ninta's gifts to Beta.                            |
| Malah:  | Oh, thanks for reminding me! It slipped my mind. She deserves a salute for standing ready to receive our daughter in her arms. |
| Muluh:  | After thanking them, what next?                              |
| Malah:  | Let's grant a wish to them. They are so deserving of it.     |
| Muluh:  | I support your decision. Ako is the loser as it is.          |
| Malah:  | That does him justice. He's a tight-fisted hypocrite. I'm unwell, he visits, talks, talks, talks and goes. A parrot at night, a parrot in daylight! What's that supposed to mean? No paracetamol tablet to soothe my pains! No droplet of mineral water for my tablets! Is that how we woo and marry someone's child? |
| Muluh:  | I don't understand him at all. Suitors swing into action. I didn't see him in any action. He's an absentee warlord. |
| Malah:  | A most ridiculous one, so to say!                            |
| Muluh:  | We should now set a date for the betrothal ceremony.         |
| Malah:  | I learnt that sooner or later Ninta will be given in marriage to an Elepe man. |
| Muluh:  | A right time to reconcile ourselves, indeed! Our children are pushing us to see fertile visions. They're ridding us of unjust guilt. |

Of what use were superior airs, by the way? Why think we're better than others? I'm a coffin maker. Do I make coffins only for one tribe? I make good cash when many people die. I have access to cold cash when people lose their lives. Anyhow, everyone is bound to die someday. I, too, will be laid in a coffin made by someone else. I jubilate when death comes aplenty. I rejoice when coffin demand rises on the market.

Someone shall rejoice to resell a coffin he got on the black market for my own dead body.

Malah:    Vanity of vanities, and boom... there goes the bell for Banta to seek peace with us. And marriage has become a solution to our conflict. Let's open our arms and embrace peace.

Muluh:    My arms are set apart. Let's give peace and love a chance till the end of time.

Malah:    Halleluiah!

**The end**

Printed in the United States
by Baker & Taylor Publisher Services